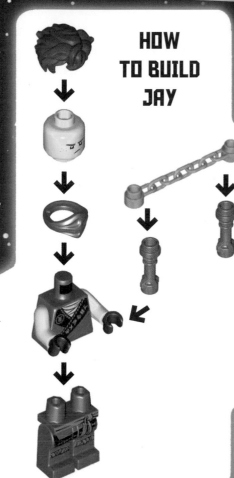

HOW TO BUILD JAY

WE'RE SEARCHING
THE MECHANIC'S HEADQUARTERS
TO FIND OUT WHY HE WANTED TO STEAL
SOME OLD TECH. LET'S GO TEAM!
WAIT—ANYONE SEEN JAY?

THE NINJA ARE TRACKING THE MECHANIC AND HIS GANG.
FOLLOW THEIR MOVEMENTS AND MARK THEIR LOCATION.

NORTH

WEST — EAST

SOUTH

1
2
3
4
5
6
7

A B C D E F G H

1. THE MECHANIC AND HIS GANG MOVED FROM SQUARE A1 BY ONE SQUARE SOUTH
   AND THEN BY TWO SQUARES EAST.
2. AT THE NEON SIGNS THEY JUMPED SOUTH TWO SQUARES ON TOP OF THE ROOF
   AND THEN RAN THREE SQUARES SOUTH.
3. NEXT, THEY SNUCK FOUR SQUARES EAST.
4. THEY MOVED THREE SQUARES NORTH, ONE WEST, ONE
   NORTH AND FINALLY TWO EAST.

2

JAY IS TRYING TO GET THROUGH THE THIRTEEN LEVELS OF THE PRIME EMPIRE. YOU CAN HELP HIM BY DRAWING STRAIGHT LINES CONNECTING ALL THE SPIDERS, ONE AFTER ANOTHER, WITHOUT TOUCHING THE WALLS IN BETWEEN.

START

COMPLETE THE GRID WITH NINJA COLORS SO THAT NONE OF THE NINJA APPEAR MORE THAN ONCE IN ANY ROW OR COLUMN.

ACCORDING TO MY CALCULATIONS . . . THIS WILL BE NO PICNIC.

CAN YOU SPOT THE MOTHERBOARD IN THIS MESS AND GET TO IT QUICKER THAN THE MECHANIC?

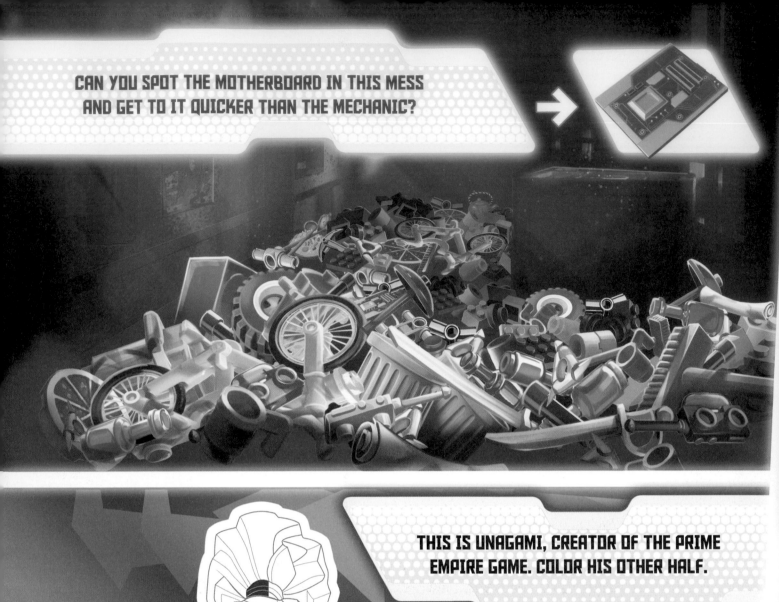

THIS IS UNAGAMI, CREATOR OF THE PRIME EMPIRE GAME. COLOR HIS OTHER HALF.

OUR NEW MYSTERIOUS OPPONENT!

HURRY UP! I NEED TO GO!

CONNECT THE DOTS TO SEE WHAT LLOYD'S VEHICLE LOOKS LIKE!

THE NINJA ARE LOOKING FOR UNAGAMI, WHO IS RUMORED TO BE HIDING ON DYER ISLAND. MOVE ALONG THE SQUARES IN THE DIRECTION INDICATED BY THE ARROWS TO REACH THE FINISH WITHOUT PASSING THROUGH ANY OF THE SQUARES MORE THAN ONCE.

START

FINISH

OPERATION DYER ISLAND

WHEN THE NINJA LINKED THE DISAPPEARANCE OF JAY WITH THE MYSTERIOUS PRIME EMPIRE VIDEO GAME, THEY WENT TO DYER ISLAND TO SEEK HELP FROM THE GAME'S CREATOR.

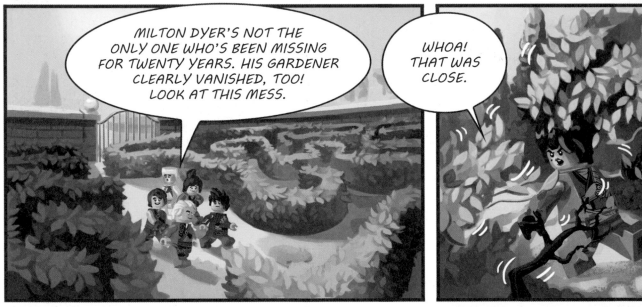

MILTON DYER'S NOT THE ONLY ONE WHO'S BEEN MISSING FOR TWENTY YEARS. HIS GARDENER CLEARLY VANISHED, TOO! LOOK AT THIS MESS.

WHOA! THAT WAS CLOSE.

STEP SLOWLY AND DELIBERATELY. YOU NEVER KNOW WHAT COULD . . .

HELP THE NINJA GET THROUGH THE HEDGE MAZE TO MILTON DYER'S MANSION.

FINISH

START

FIND ZANE'S BELONGINGS IN THE MAZE.

8

STEP ON THE ROCKS FOLLOWING THE ARROW SEQUENCE
BELOW TO HELP KAI REACH THE HOUSE.

FINISH

START

IN EACH ROW, ONE OF THE WEAPONS IS DIFFERENT
FROM THE OTHERS. FIND AND MARK IT.

CAN YOU SPOT THESE DECORATIVE ELEMENTS ON MY OUTFITS?

FINISH JAY'S AVATAR BY COMPLETING THE EMPTY SPACES ON BOTH PICTURES.

COLOR IN JAY'S AWESOME GUITAR!

THE GAME
BY TRACEY WEST

Bam!

Kai kicked in the door of the abandoned video arcade. The light from the blue neon sign outside cast an eerie glow on the place. Old arcade consoles and pinball machines filled the room. He and the other ninja pushed aside cobwebs as they stepped inside.

"Old-school video games?!" Jay said. "This is awesome!"

"Do you really think this is the Mechanic's hideout?" Jay wondered.

"He was running this way when we caught him," Nya pointed out.

Lloyd nodded. "Right now this is our only lead," he said. "We need to find out what the Mechanic is up to. Let's look for clues."

"I'm going to play everything!" Jay exclaimed before calming down. "I mean, I'll look for clues over here."

Cole picked up a metal robo-arm and waved it around the room. "If we're looking for robo-arms, we don't have to look far," he said. Mechanical robo-arms were everywhere — hanging from the ceiling, stacked on shelves, and strewn across the floor.

Lloyd shuddered. "Super creepy," he said.

"I do not see what is super creepy about a robo-arm," Zane said defensively.

"They're not creepy when they're *attached* to a robot," Jay said. "But having piles of them is just weird."

Kai leapt over to the staircase. "I'll check upstairs!" he announced.

Jay spotted something under a pile of junk.

"Look, it's a computer!" he cried. "Maybe it contains the files for a secret plan or something."

He pulled it out and set it up on one of the old machines. Cole, Nya, Lloyd, and Zane gathered around to watch. Jay plugged it in, and the monitor glowed. Music played, and words popped up on the screen.

Do you want to play the amazing robo-arms?

"Cool, it's a game!" Jay said. He searched around. "There's got to be some controllers somewhere — here they are!"

He picked up a controller and pressed the button.

How many players?

"Five!" Jay exclaimed.

Cole, Nya, Lloyd, and Zane each picked up a controller. A robot with five arms appeared on the screen. "I don't see why this primitive robot needs five arms," Zane remarked. "I only need two."

Jay moved his joystick, and one of the robo-arms moved. "I think we each control an arm," he said.

On the screen, a big clown with a red nose appeared.

LEVEL ONE: TAKE DOWN THE CLOWN

"Let's get him!" Lloyd cried.

Meanwhile, upstairs, Kai was frowning.

"Nothing up here but a pile of robo-arms," he said, looking at tube-like arms with grabby claws for hands.

Kai moved to leave, but suddenly bright lights began to flash. Loud disco music started playing. The door to the room slammed shut!

"What's going on?" Kai wondered.

Five of the robo-arms came to life and lunged at him!

Downstairs, the other ninja frantically pressed their controller buttons.

Bam! Pow! Boom! Wham! They lobbed punches at the clown on the screen.

"Is this clown gonna fight back, or what?" Jay asked.

"It looks like he's . . . dancing," Nya said.

Upstairs, Kai dodged the swinging robo-arms.

"Ow! Ouch! Quit it!" he cried, as he jumped to avoid the attack.

One robo-arm lunged at him, and Kai grabbed it in midair. He slammed it on the floor. The arm twitched, sparked, and then stopped moving.

"One down!" Kai cheered.

Downstairs, Zane watched his robo-arm stop moving. He put down his controller. "It appears that I am out."

"Maybe this guy isn't such a clown after all," Nya said. "Take that. Pow!"

Nya's robo-arm reached out to pinch the clown's big red nose.

Upstairs, one of the mechanical robo-arms reached for Kai's nose. He gripped the arm before it made contact.

"Hands off!" Kai yelled, and he swung the arm over his head. Then he launched it into the wall. *Crash!*

Downstairs, Nya's robo-arm stopped moving on the screen. "I'm out."

On the screen, the clown stamped his feet angrily. *Whack!* He kicked the robot.

Cole turned to Lloyd. "Robo double punch!"

Pow! Pow! Cole and Lloyd attacked the clown together.

Upstairs, Kai blocked the double punches with karate chops.

Bam! Bam!

Cole and Lloyd's robo-arms stopped working.

"Looks like it's just me," Jay said, and the screen flashed.

Second level! One-on-one!

A new, bigger robot avatar appeared on the screen. This one had ten robo-arms.

Kai leaned against the wall, panting. One last robo-arm hovered in the air.

Just one more to go, he thought. But then, to his horror, the whole pile of arms came to life!

"Woo-hoo!" Jay cheered downstairs. "I can control all the arms at once! Take that, clownie!"

Kai had had enough.

"Ninjaaaaaaaaago!"

He spun around the room in a whirlwind, destroying the ten

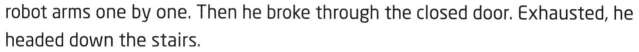

robot arms one by one. Then he broke through the closed door. Exhausted, he headed down the stairs.

Kai found Jay and the others in front of a computer monitor. His eyes widened as he saw the ten-armed robot avatar on the screen. Then it dawned on him: His friends had been controlling the robo-arms through the video game!

"I almost got him!" Jay was saying, and then he spun around. "Hey Kai, we discovered an awesome game. I almost beat it. You want to play with us?"

"I have a better idea," Kai said. "I'll play the game while you go upstairs and check out the interesting things I found there!"

1

2

3

4

5

6

18

CROSS OUT THE PAIRS OF IDENTICAL GAME CONSOLES. THE CONSOLE WITHOUT A PAIR CONTAINS THE PRIME EMPIRE GAME.

CRACK THE NUMBER CODES BY WRITING THE CORRECT NUMBERS IN THE EMPTY BOXES–THIS MIGHT HELP YOU INITIATE THE GAME.

SPOT THE HATS AND ROBO-ARMS FROM THE BOX BELOW ON THE WALL OF THE MECHANIC'S HIDEOUT.

CRACK THE MECHANIC'S DOOR CODE. COMPLETE THE GRID SO THAT THE TOTAL OF THE NUMBERS FROM TWO NEIGHBORING SQUARES APPEARS IN THE SQUARE DIRECTLY ABOVE THEM.

9   5

7   2   3   1   4

START

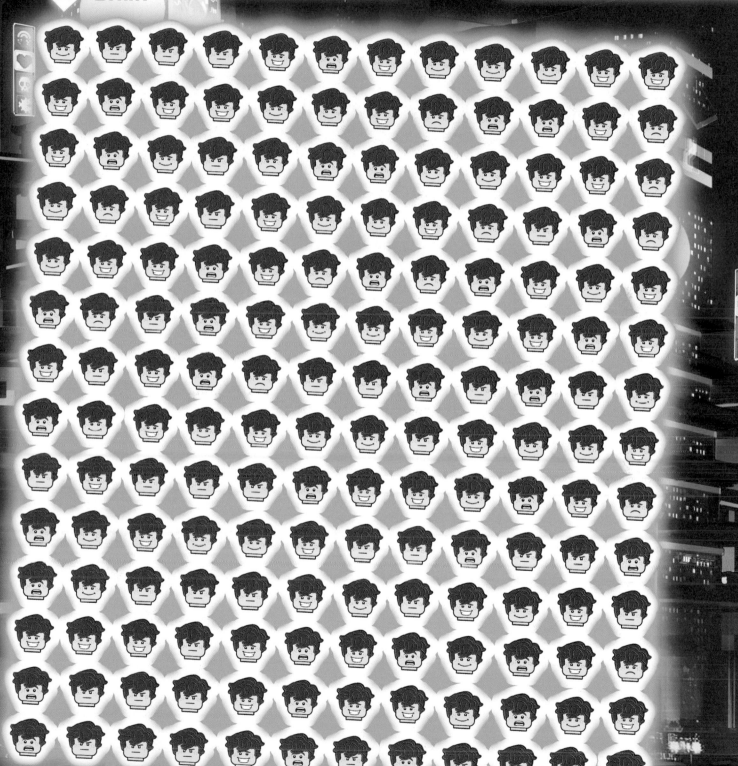

FINISH

UNSCRAMBLE THE NAMES OF THE CHARACTERS IN THE PORTRAITS.

NILMOT REDY

MILTON DYER

CEANIMCH

_____

GAUNAIM

_____

IXPLA

_____

ANPITAC OTOS

_____

EZAN

_____

HELP COLE LEAD THE ROBOT THROUGH THE SPACE SPIDERS. CHOOSE THE CORRECT SEQUENCE OF ARROW MOVEMENTS.

HELP NYA COMPLETE A LEVEL OF THE GAME. MOVE HORIZONTALLY AND VERTICALLY, COLLECTING ALL THE SHURIKENS ON THE WAY.

YOU CAN STEP ON EACH SQUARE ONLY ONCE. YOU MUST AVOID SQUARES WITH SKULLS.

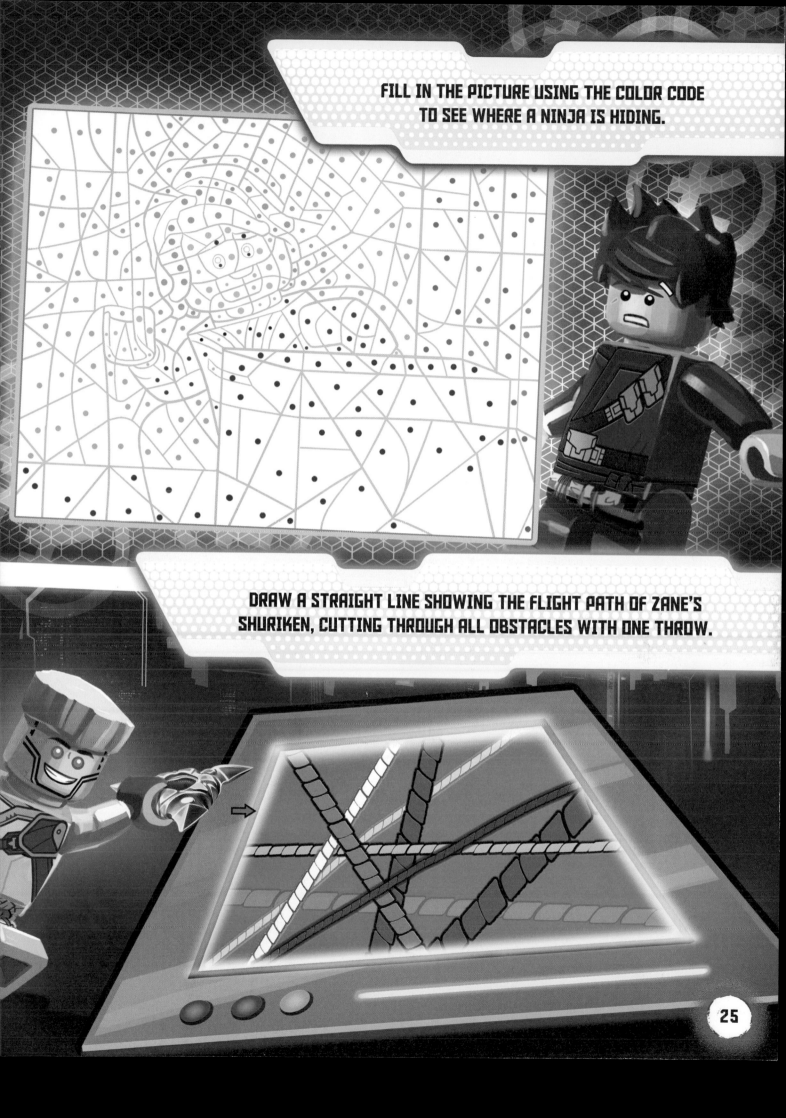

FILL IN THE PICTURE USING THE COLOR CODE TO SEE WHERE A NINJA IS HIDING.

DRAW A STRAIGHT LINE SHOWING THE FLIGHT PATH OF ZANE'S SHURIKEN, CUTTING THROUGH ALL OBSTACLES WITH ONE THROW.

TO WHAT END?

MORE AND MORE PEOPLE PLAYING A MYSTERIOUS VIDEO GAME ARE DISAPPEARING IN NINJAGO CITY. WHILE THE YOUNG NINJA ARE TRYING TO SOLVE THE MYSTERY, A CERTAIN CRIMINAL IS SENT TO KRYPTORIUM PRISON (NOT FOR THE FIRST TIME).

WELCOME BACK, MECHANIC. WE KEPT YOUR USUAL CELL FOR YOU!

SOON I'LL BE ON TOP AGAIN.

YEAH. TOP BUNK, IF YOU'RE LUCKY.

WHAT'S THIS?

THERE'S SOMETHING WRONG WITH THE SECURITY SYSTEM.

UNAGAMI REQUIRES YOUR ASSISTANCE. WILL YOU SERVE UNAGAMI?

YES! I WON'T LET YOU DOWN.

WHAT'S GOING ON?!

IF YOU FAIL UNAGAMI A SECOND TIME, IT WILL BE GAME OVER.

CAPTAIN SOTO! ULTRAVIOLET! ALL OF YOU! COME WITH ME. WORK FOR UNAGAMI, AND YOU WILL BE REWARDED HANDSOMELY.

I'VE BEEN DIGGING A TUNNEL EVERY NIGHT FOR SIX MONTHS! I TRADED THIRTY DINNERS FOR THIS SPOON. AND TO WHAT END?

ON THE OTHER HAND, IF THERE'S A LOUDSPEAKER THAT TAKES CARE OF THINGS . . . HEY, CAN YOU HEAR ME? CAN YOU GET ME TWO HAMBURGERS?

FIND AND MARK THE MISTAKE ON EACH OF
CAPTAIN SOTO'S PORTRAITS.

THE MECHANIC, CAPTAIN SOTO, AND ULTRAVIOLET HAVE BROKEN OUT OF JAIL.
ADD THE NUMBERS ALONG EACH PATH. THE SMALLEST SUM WILL MARK THE PATH
THAT LLOYD WILL TAKE TO CATCH THEM.

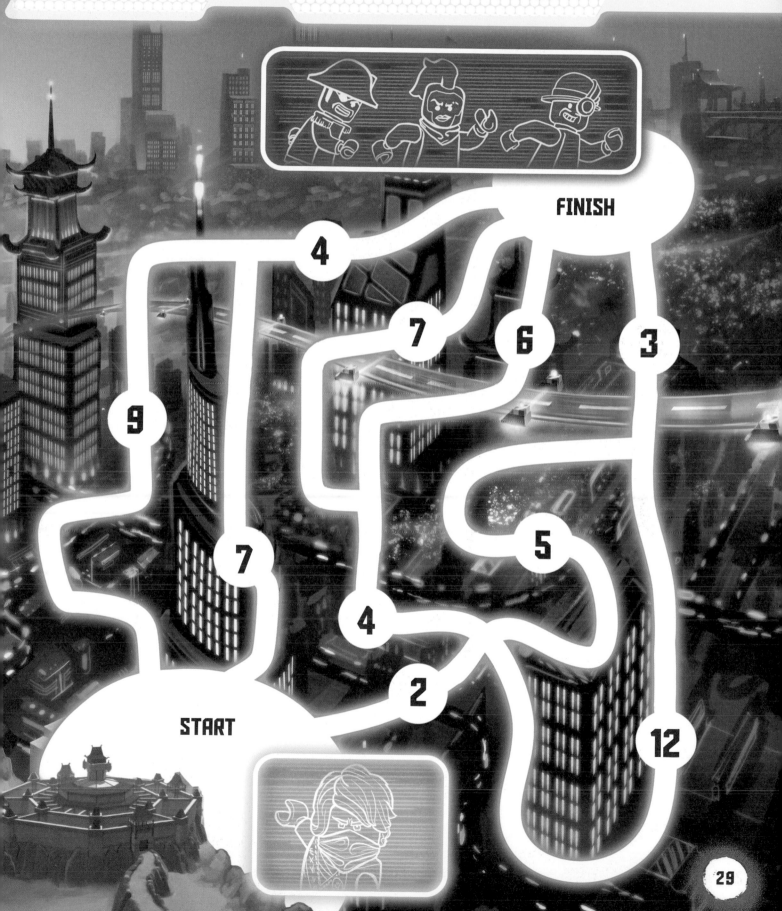

FINISH

4

7 6 3

9

7 5

4

2

START

12

LOOK AT THE ILLUSTRATION, THEN ANSWER THE QUESTIONS.

1. THERE ARE ONLY FIVE NINJA IN THE PICTURE.   TRUE/FALSE
2. THE CHEST KAI IS HIDING BEHIND IS RED.   TRUE/FALSE
3. COLE IS STANDING CLOSEST TO NYA.   TRUE/FALSE
4. THE KATANA LLOYD IS HOLDING IS SILVER.   TRUE/FALSE
5. THERE IS SOMEONE ELSE IN THE ROOM APART FROM THE NINJA.   TRUE/FALSE

TRY SPELLING THE NAMES OF ALL THE NINJA WITH THE LETTERS BELOW, USING EACH LETTER ONLY ONCE. WHOSE NAME IS MISSING?

A D A N O L A Z Y K I O L E N E C Y L

1. NYA   2. . . . . . .   3. . . . . . .   4. . . . . . .   5. . . . . . .   6. . . . . . . ?

ANSWERS

p. 2
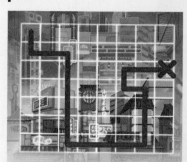

p. 3

p. 3

p. 4

p. 4
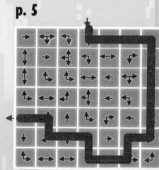

p. 5
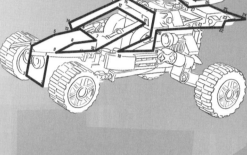

p. 9

p. 5
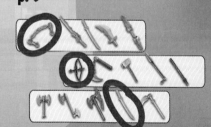

p. 8

p. 9

p. 10

p. 11

p. 12

p. 18

p. 19

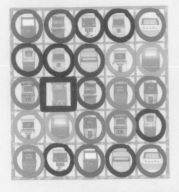

p. 19

p. 20

p. 22

MECHANIC, UNAGAMI, PIXAL, CAPTAIN SOTO, ZANE

p. 20

41

23   18

14   9   9

9   5   4   5

7   2   3   1   4

p. 21

p. 22

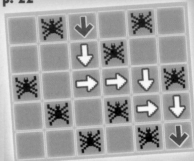

C ↓ ↓ → → ↓ → ↓ ↓

p. 23

p. 24

p. 25

p. 25

p. 28

p. 29

p. 30

1. FALSE
2. FALSE
3. FALSE
4. TRUE
5. FALSE

p. 30

NYA, KAI, LLOYD, ZANE, COLE, JAY IS MISSING